DATE DUE		
OCT 30 '93	JUL 0 8 1999	JUN 2 2 2009
AUG 21 '95	JUL 1 9 2000	JUN 1 5 2010
OCT 25 '95	NOV 2 2 2000	JUL 0 8 2010
OCT 30 '95	MAR 0 7 2001	AUG 1 7 2010
MAR 6- '96	MAY 0 9 2001	AUG 0 5 2011
AUG 14 '96	NOV 1 8 2003	
MAR 2 2 1997	OCT. 1 8 2004	JUN 2 7 2012
MAY 2 3 1998	FEB. 0 9 2005	JUL 0 5 2012
JUL 1 3 1998	SEP. 2 6 2005	AUG 1 5 2012
AUG 1 2 1998	NOV. 3 0 2005	SEP 1 0 2012
DEC 0 9 1998	APR. 0 5 2007	AUG 0 9 2018
MAR 1 0 1999	FEB 1 1 2009	

The Too Hot Day

by Beverly Komoda

HarperCollins*Publishers*

THE TOO HOT DAY
Copyright © 1991 by Beverly Komoda
Printed in the U.S.A. All rights reserved.
Typography by David Saylor
10 9 8 7 6 5 4 3 2 1
First Edition

Library of Congress Cataloging-in-Publication Data
Komoda, Beverly.
    The too hot day / by Beverly Komoda.
        p.   cm.
    Summary: Mama takes her little rabbits for a walk to the lake on a
very hot summer day.
    ISBN 0-06-021611-5. — ISBN 0-06-021612-3 (lib. bdg.)
    [1. Rabbits—Fiction.   2. Summer—Fiction.]   I. Title.
PZ7.K8348Ho   1991   90-1620
[E]—dc20   CIP
                                                         AC

The art in this book was prepared using pen and ink,
colored pencils, and watercolors.

16154

For Lisa and David Hambro

It was a very hot day.

"Mama, we are so hot, we might melt!" said Milly.

"I think I already have," said Herbert.

"Me too," said Mac.

Minny and Vinny were too hot to move.

"Think about cold things,"
said Mama.

"Orange juice!" said Mac.

"Snowballs!" said Milly.

"Ears!" said Herbert.

Mama laughed. "Ears aren't cold,"
she said.

"Mine are when I take them outside
in the winter," said Herbert.

"Let's go for a cool walk," said Mama.

"A walk? *Hooray!!!*" shouted Herbert, Mac, and Milly.

"I'll get Minny and Vinny's stroller," said Mac.

Herbert walked very slowly.

"I'm *still* hot," he said.

"We can walk in the shade," said Milly.

"I'm thirsty!" said Herbert.

"We're thirsty! We're thirsty!" shouted Mac and Milly.

"Settle down now and don't fuss," said Mama.

"Who would like some nice cold juice?"
asked Mama.

"We would! We would!" said
Herbert, Mac, and Milly.

"Let's drink our juice by the lake,"
said Milly.

"We can sit in the shade,"
said Herbert.

"All right," said Mama.

"The lake looks very cool," said Mac.

"Papa would like this," said Milly.

"Yes, he would," said Mama.

"We can tell him about it at dinner tonight,"
said Herbert.

Mac finished his juice first.

"Let's race our cups in the lake!" he said.

Minny and Vinny wanted to see
the cup race.
Mama started to push the stroller
down to the lake.
The hill was too steep!
Mama slipped.
The stroller rolled away.
"Oh, my!!" cried Mama.

Herbert, Mac, and Milly jumped up.
"E-ee-eee-eeep!" they squealed.
They stopped the stroller just in time
but it pushed them into the lake!
Splash!
Mama came sliding down the hill.

"Oh, my dears!" said Mama.
"Thank you so much!
We'd better go right home."

Squish! Squish! went their wet shoes.

Suddenly, rain began to fall.

"Mama, you will be as wet as we are," said Milly.

They hurried home.

"I know," said Milly. "Let's save some rain to show
Papa when he gets home."
They left their juice cups on the grass.

Rain fell all afternoon.

But when Papa came home from work,
the sun was shining again.

Herbert, Mac, and Milly ran outside.

Mac said, "Papa! Guess what we did today!"

"Tell me," said Papa.

"We went for a walk because it was too hot," said Mac.

"Minny and Vinny almost fell into the lake."

"But we stopped them," said Herbert.

"Then it rained," said Milly.

"We saved the rain to show you."

Papa looked.

"Why, that is the nicest rain I have ever seen!"
he said.

And he gave them all a hug and a kiss.